Uncle Alonzo's Beard

Written by Emma King-Farlow
& illustrated by Anna Laura Cantone

meadowside

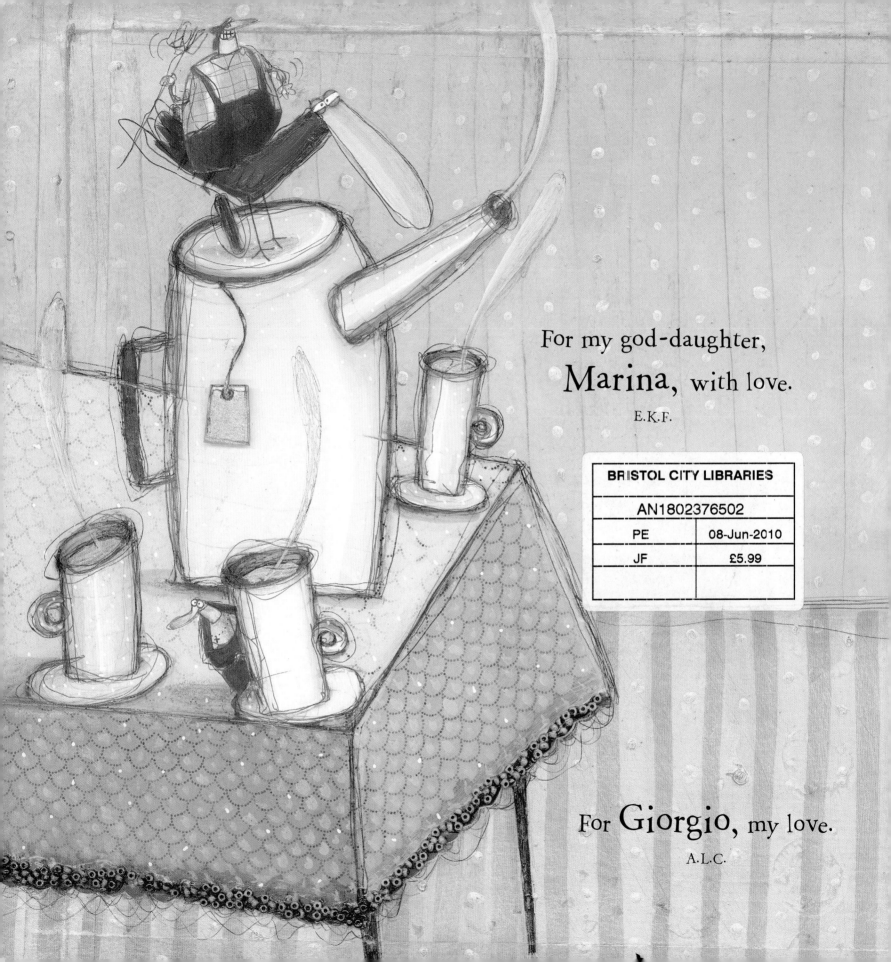

For my god-daughter,
Marina, with love.
E.K.F.

For **Giorgio,** my love.
A.L.C.

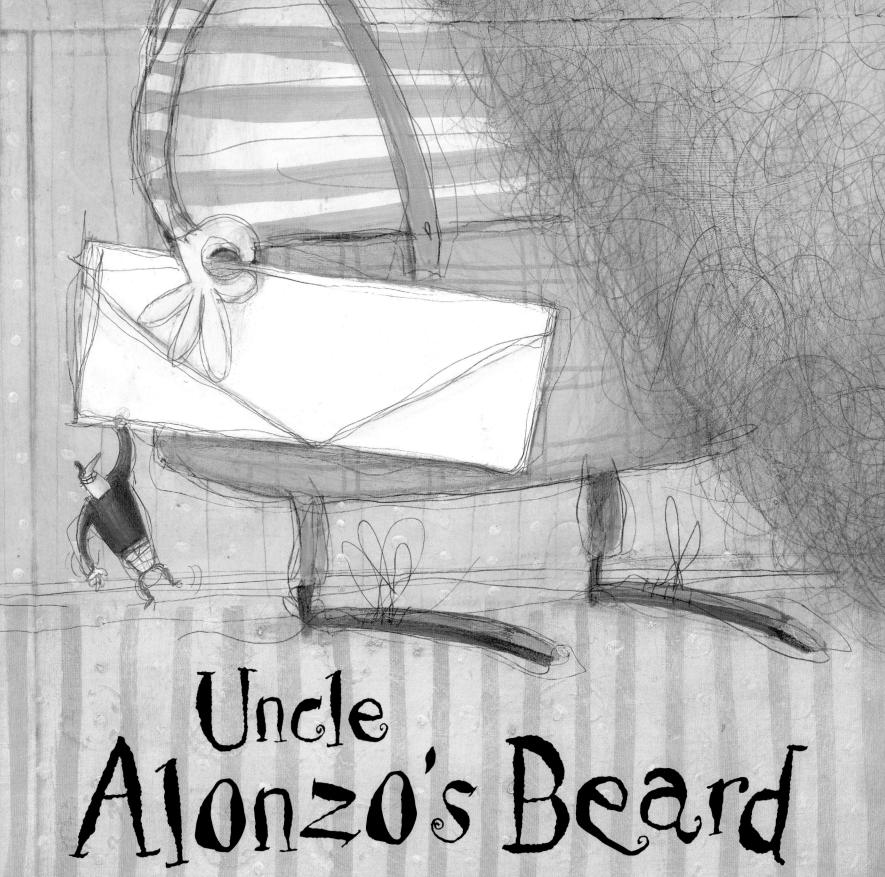

Uncle Alonzo's Beard

Written by Emma King-Farlow & illustrated by Anna Laura Cantone

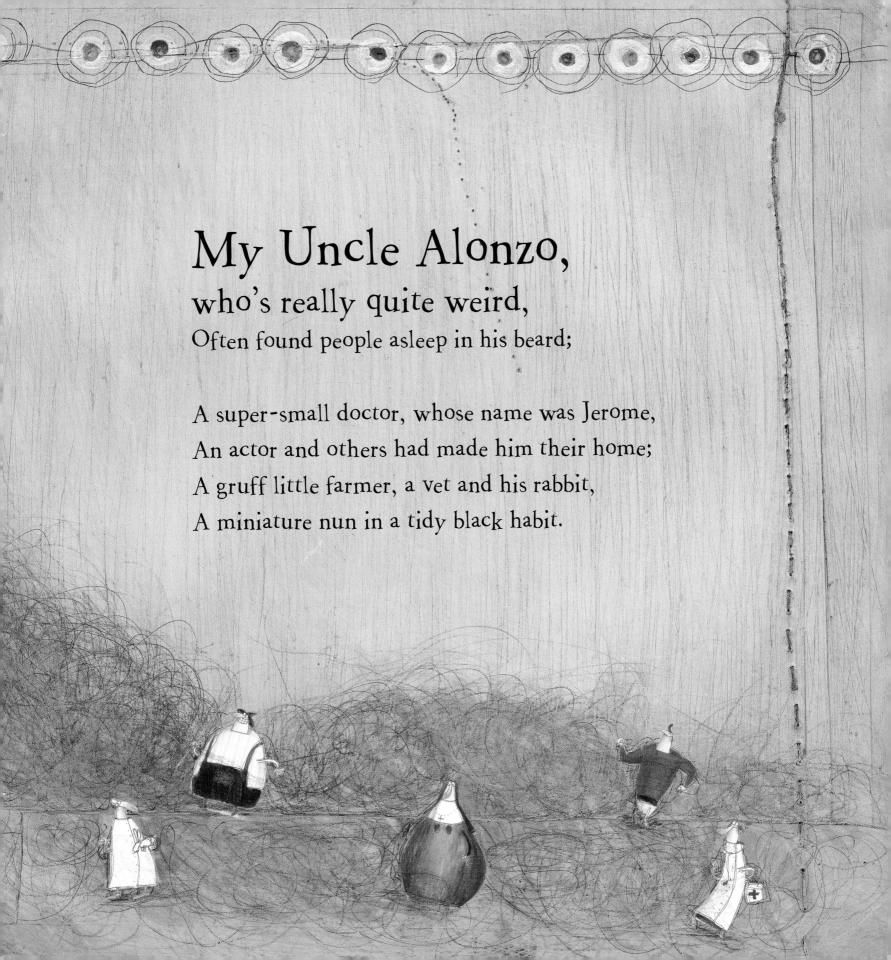

My Uncle Alonzo,

who's really quite weird,
Often found people asleep in his beard;

A super-small doctor, whose name was Jerome,
An actor and others had made him their home;
A gruff little farmer, a vet and his rabbit,
A miniature nun in a tidy black habit.

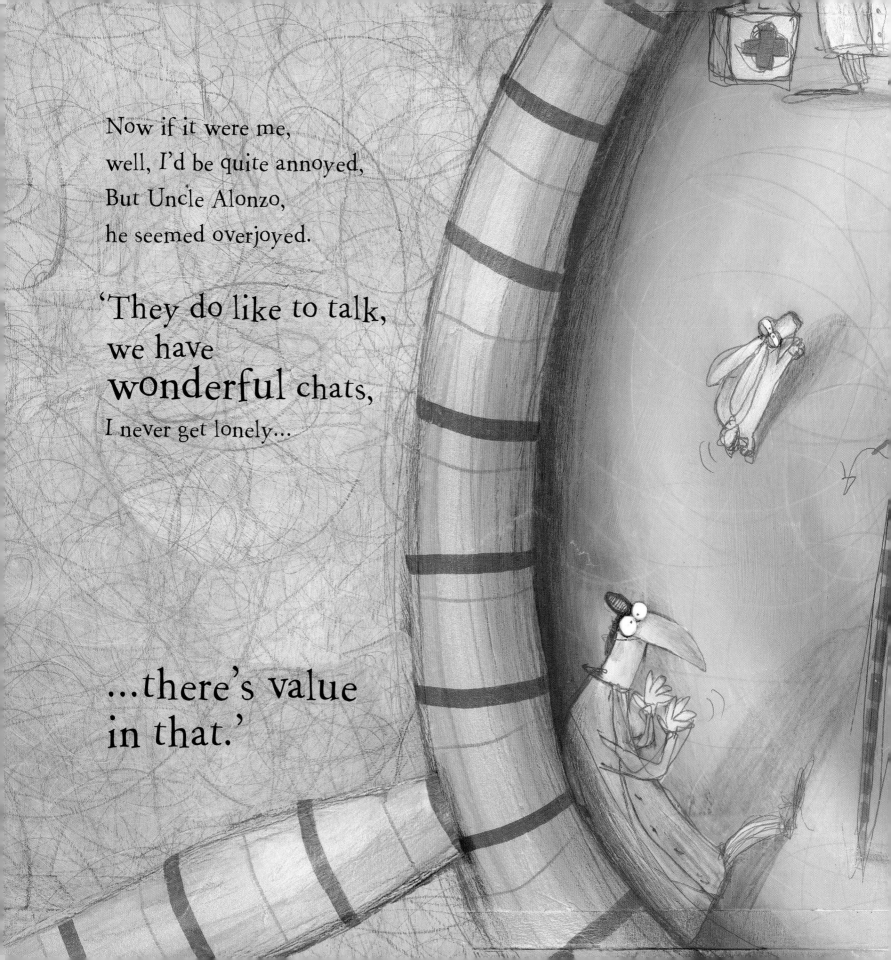

Now if it were me,
well, I'd be quite annoyed,
But Uncle Alonzo,
he seemed overjoyed.

'They do like to talk,
we have
wonderful chats,
I never get lonely...

...there's value
in that.'

I smiled and I nodded but couldn't agree;
It's ten years ago since the beard

passed his knee!

He still couldn't cut it –
not even a trim...

Since so many people
relied upon him.

But only last Tuesday
there came a **big** change.
It all started off with a smell that was strange.
With this curious smell came a trickle of smoke;
Alonzo knew instantly this was no joke.

As a flame flickered out
he let out a
yelp!

Then he picked
up the phone
to call for some help.

'Good afternoon, sir,' trilled the shrill operator,

'I'm quite busy knitting. Can't this wait 'til later?'

'No, my good lady,
I fear it cannot.
My beard is on fire
and it's growing
quite
hot!'

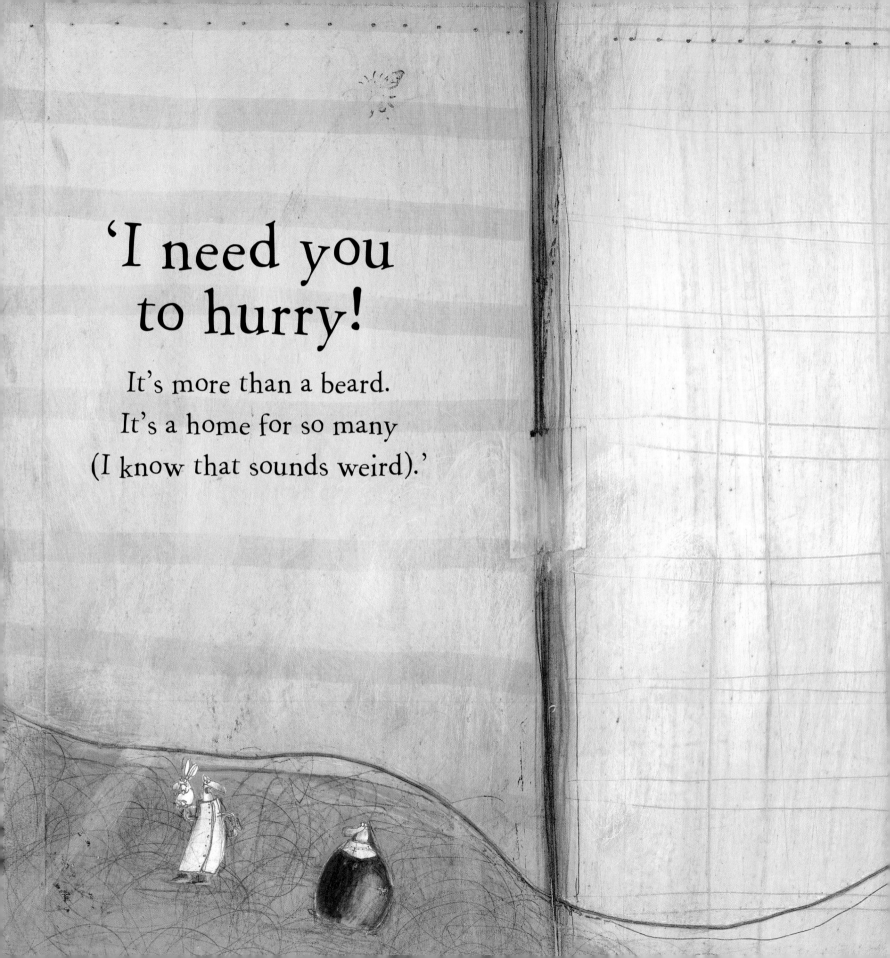

'I need you
to hurry!

It's more than a beard.
It's a home for so many
(I know that sounds weird).'

A little time later the firemen came...

...And in a few moments
had put out each flame.
The doctor, the farmer,
the vet and the nun,
All gave a huge cheer
once the rescue
was done.

But as the smoke cleared
and the damage was seen,
Alonzo's small tenants,
began to turn **green.**

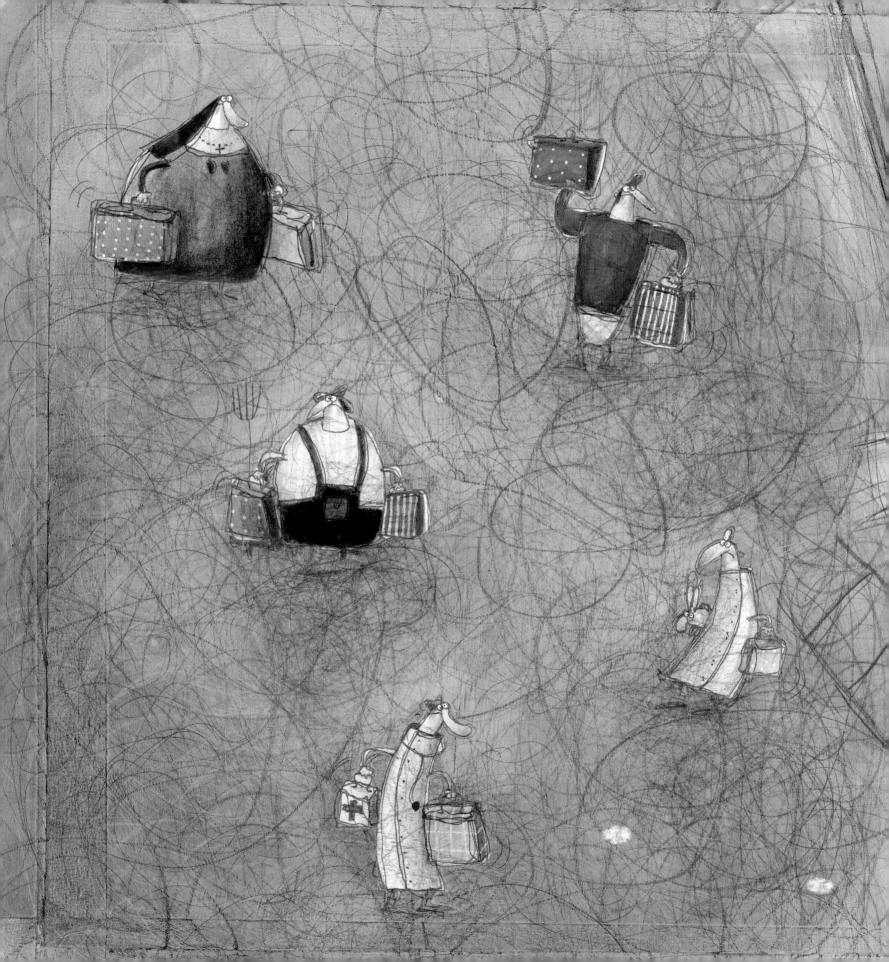

The chief fire-fighter confirmed their worst fears
When presenting his safety report on the beard.

'I'm sorry,' the man said,
'this beard is too mangled:
The few bits not burned are
impossibly tangled.

Since this smouldering beard's
now in such bad repair,

I can't see how
anyone
wants to live there!'

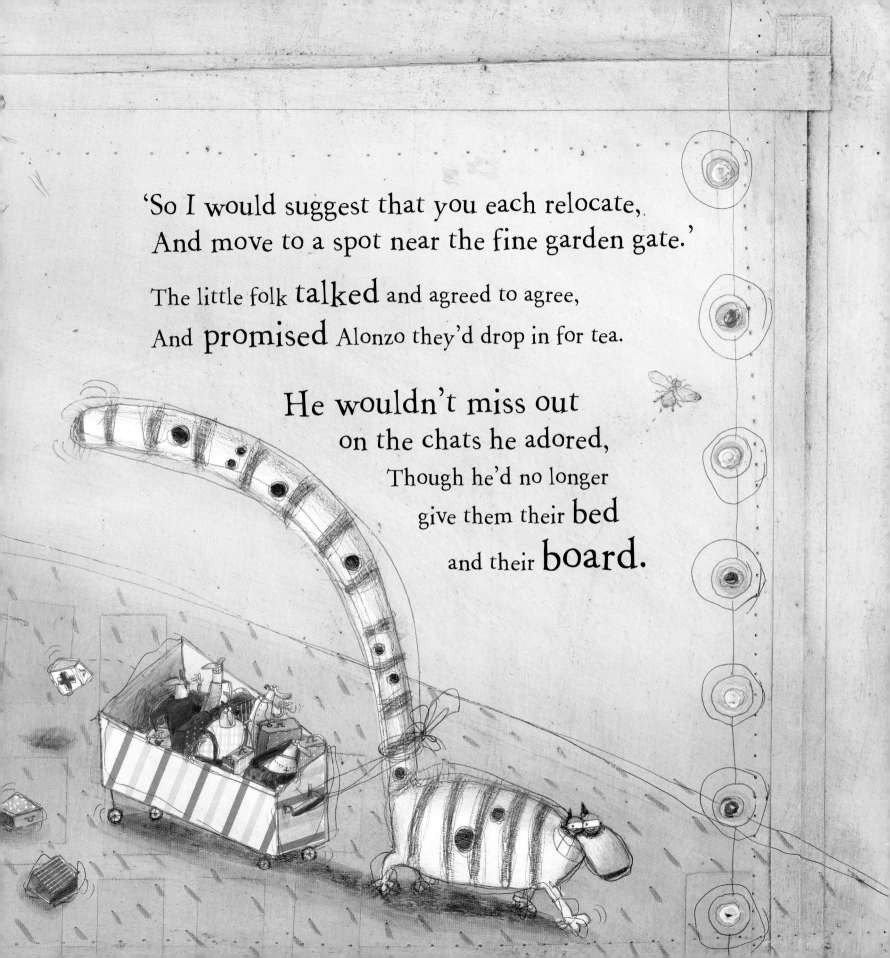

'So I would suggest that you each relocate,
And move to a spot near the fine garden gate.'

The little folk **talked** and agreed to agree,
And **promised** Alonzo they'd drop in for tea.

He wouldn't miss out
on the chats he adored,
Though he'd no longer
give them their **bed**
and their **board.**

Alonzo said,

'Marvellous!
Let's start right away,
For though I will miss you,
I've something to say;
I've waited so long and for so many years

To finally find I can shave off

my beard!'

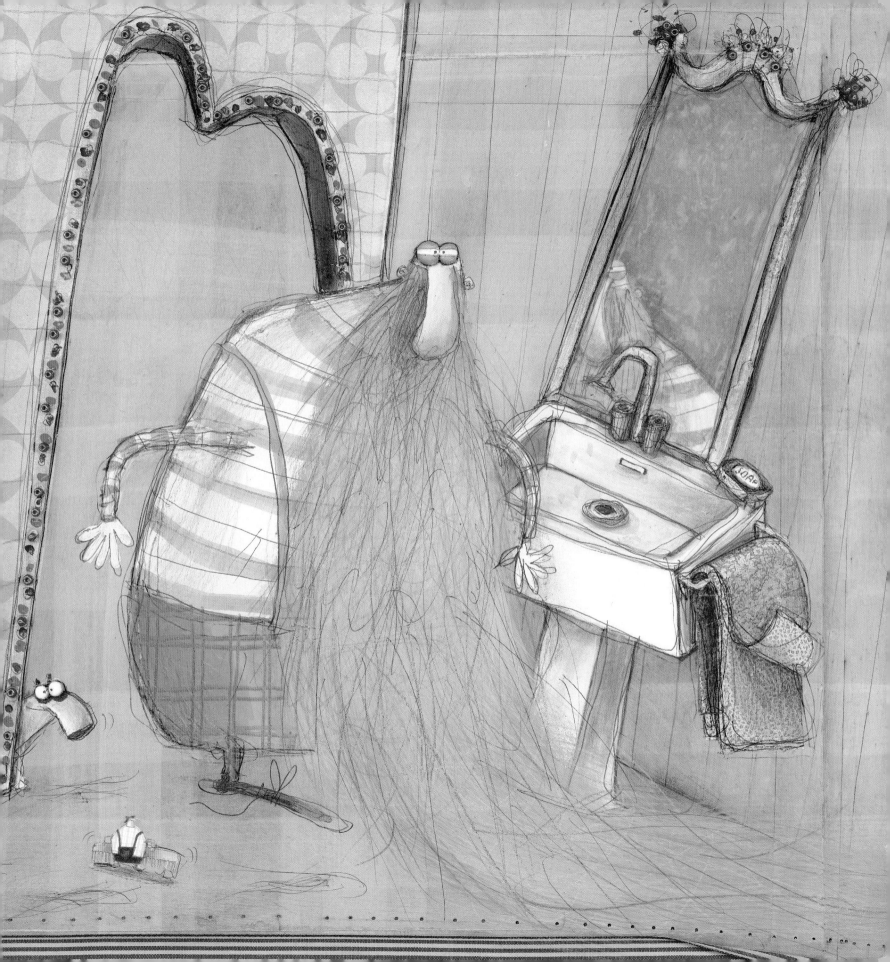

So the **fire**,
as you see,
brought the best
of all ends
For my Uncle Alonzo
and each of his friends.

They all loved the garden
once they had moved in,

And **Alonzo**,
he treasured his
newly...

...smooth
skin!

First published in 2006
by Meadowside Children's Books
185 Fleet Street
London EC4A 2HS

A CIP catalogue record for this book
is available from the British Library

ISBN 10 Hbk 1-84539-212-4
ISBN 10 Pbk 1-84539-196-9
ISBN 13 Hbk 978-1-84539-212-3
ISBN 13 Pbk 978-1-84539-196-6

10 9 8 7 6 5 4 3 2 1
Printed in China